A NOTE ABOUT THE STORY

The first "strand" of this tale was handed to me on a piece of yellow typing paper by my friend Doug Duchin. In a few sentences he had sketched a Persian legend that had long been associated with a sixteenth-century Mamluk carpet, explaining its pattern, which looked like a landscape strewn with jewels. I put the tale in a drawer, where it sat for many years.

Then, cleaning house one day, I came across the tale again. Once more it piqued my interest, but this time I decided to retell and expand it for Whitebird Books, which had recently been established. After much research and polishing, the manuscript was ready.

At about this time I happened to be at a Society of Children's Book Writers conference in California, evaluating artists' portfolios. I saw the work of Claire Ewart and was very excited about it. Here was a chance for me to do something I had always discussed with my editor and mentor, Margaret Frith, but had never done: ask someone else to illustrate one of my stories. And no author could ask for a more talented interpreter.

Before even beginning her sketches, Claire spent a great deal of time learning about Persian art and history. She studied Persian miniaturists, and even traveled overseas to see the architecture up close and witness carpets being made. All of which gives an added richness to this tale of treasure lost, and treasure regained.

—*Tomie dePaola, Creative Director*
WHITEBIRD BOOKS

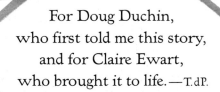

For Doug Duchin,
who first told me this story,
and for Claire Ewart,
who brought it to life. — T.dP.

For Helen,
who believed in me,
and thanks also to
Kathy I. and Kathy C. — C.E.

Text copyright © 1993 by Tomie dePaola
Illustrations copyright © 1993 by Claire Ewart
All rights reserved. This book, or parts thereof, may not be reproduced
in any form without permission in writing from the publisher.
G. P. Putnam's Sons, a division of The Putnam & Grosset Group,
200 Madison Avenue, New York, NY 10016. Published simultaneously in Canada.
Printed in Hong Kong by South China Printing Co. (1988) Ltd.
Book design by Gunta Alexander. The text is set in Hadriano.
Library of Congress Cataloging-in-Publication Data
dePaola, Tomie. The legend of the persian carpet / Tomie dePaola; illustrated by Claire Ewart.   p.   cm.
Summary: Tells how a Persian carpet was created to replace King Balash's lost treasure.
[1. Folklore—Iran. 2. Carpets—Folklore.] I. Ewart, Claire, ill.
II. Title.   PZ8.1.D438Le   1993   398.2—dc20   [E]   91-45816 CIP AC
ISBN 0-399-22415-7
1 3 5 7 9 10 8 6 4 2
First Impression

The Legend of the Persian Carpet

RETOLD BY **TOMIE** DE**PAOLA**

ILLUSTRATED BY **CLAIRE EWART**

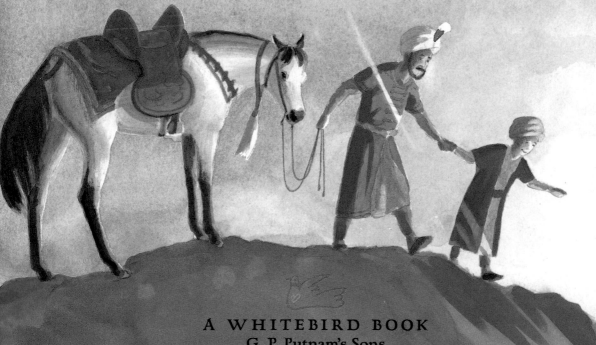

A **WHITEBIRD** BOOK

G. P. Putnam's Sons
New York

Many, many years ago, in the land once called Persia, there lived a kind and wise king, who was much loved by his people.

He lived in a white stone palace of many rooms, surrounded by gardens filled with flowers and fruit trees and sparkling fountains. King Balash had everything a man could desire.

But his most prized possession was a large diamond. This diamond was set on a special pedestal and was so beautiful and so bright that it filled not only the room it was in but all the surrounding rooms with a million rainbows.

King Balash was not a selfish man. He loved and trusted his people so much that he kept no guards near the diamond. Every afternoon, when the sun was just right, and until it set, the king opened the doors of his palace. Anyone who wished could come to see the walls of the room painted with the diamond's light.

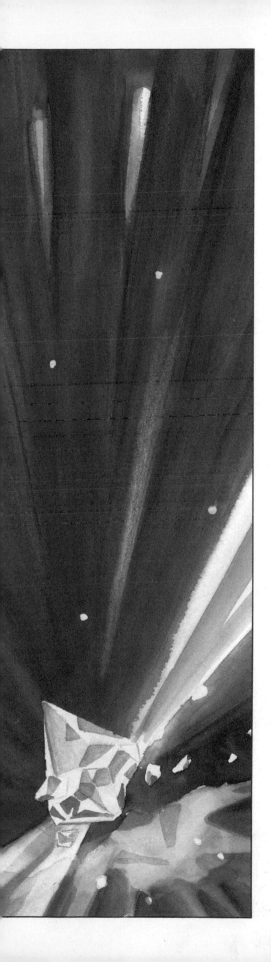

One day at dusk, as the crowds were leaving, a stranger to the kingdom slipped in among the visitors and stole the diamond. Like the wind, the thief raced his horse across the rocky plain toward the desert and the setting sun. But the horse stumbled, the diamond fell from the thief's hand, and it shattered on the rocks. The setting sun shone bloodred on the fragments and reflected a million sunsets into the thief's eyes. He staggered off empty-handed, cursing his luck and rubbing his eyes.

Now it was King Balash's custom to spend the time of the rising sun in the hall of the diamond with its amazing reflections. But instead of a million rainbows, all that greeted the king was the empty pedestal and a room filled with shadows and gloom.

"Call my people!" ordered the king.
"I must tell them of this tragedy. They
must help me find our treasure."

The people set out and soon a small boy named Payam, who was an apprentice in the Street of the Weavers, came to the rocky place. The morning sun shot through the diamond fragments and dazzled Payam with such a sight that he couldn't believe his eyes. Off he ran to the palace and was brought before the king.

"And there, O King," said Payam, "among all the rocks, is the diamond, broken into a thousand pieces, sparkling in the sun, reflecting all the colors of the rainbow on the ground."

"I must see for myself," said the king. "Go with me."

And when they reached the place, King Balash was so overwhelmed by the carpet of diamonds that he sat down and said, "I shall always stay here. I shall never enter the dark palace again."

"But Sire," cried Payam, "you can't! Who shall rule the kingdom? Who shall guide the people?"

But King Balash didn't listen. He stared at the shimmering light, lost in his own thoughts.

The people were all in confusion. Without a leader, they and their homes could be attacked by any robber-king from the desert. Their very lives were in danger.

Payam sat and thought. He called all the other young apprentices together.

"We must help our king and our people," Payam told them. "We must make a carpet as miraculous as the one our king stares at on the rocky plain. We must all work together."

The apprentices agreed. And so did the master weavers and dyers of silk threads. Everyone set to work.

Payam went to King Balash.

"Please, Sire, come back and sit on the throne for a year and a day," Payam said. "If we cannot fill the room with color and light in that time, then we will accept our fate and live without a king. A year and a day."

It was the least he could do for his people. So King Balash agreed.

Day and night they all worked, spin-
ning, dyeing, weaving on the large rug
loom. And in a year and a day, the carpet
was finished.

The workers carried the carpet to the palace and into the dark hall where the diamond had rested. With a flourish, they unrolled it before the king.

Suddenly the room was once more filled with the colors of the rainbow. Reds, golds, blues, and greens of the silk carpet glowed on the floor, reflecting color off the walls and the ceiling. Once more, the room was filled with light and King Balash and his people were happy.

And happiest of all were Payam and
the other apprentices, for they had not
only saved their kingdom, but had made
the most beautiful carpet in the world.